The short, tragic life of Leo the marsupial lion

by John Long

with illustrations by Jill Ruse

WESTERN AUSTRALIAN MUSEUM

Contents

Darwin
Australia
Brisbane
Nullarbor Plain
Perth
Adelaide
Sydney
Melbourne
Hobart

Introduction

Today the Nullarbor Plain is a vast, flat area of southern Australia spanning the border between Western Australia and South Australia. Its Latin name 'Nullarbor' means 'no trees' (null arbor), as hardly any trees grow there; mostly small saltbush, blue bush and other prickly shrubs.

The Nullarbor Plain is made up of limestone rock that was formed at the bottom of the sea about 20 million years ago. The mixing of freshwater and salty water deep underground gradually formed large caves within the limestone rock.

Today the Nullarbor Plain is littered with thousands of caves. Some of these caves are gigantic caverns that could contain a football field. While many are dry caves, others hold vast subterranean lakes.

Most of the animals that live in this region today are well adapted to the harsh climate of the area. In summer it can be scorching hot and very dry. In winter it can sometimes rain like an ocean falling on you.

Western grey kangaroos live on the Nullarbor, alongside a small population of hairy-nosed wombats. There are many smaller mammals as well, like hopping mice, and some small bandicoots. Many kinds of birds live there too, ranging from the giant wedge-tailed eagle and brush-turkey, through to a variety of colourful parrots, finches and honeyeaters.

Wedge-tailed Eagle
(Aquila audax)
Mulga Parrot
(Psephotus varius)
Dingo
(Canis lupus dingo)
Fords Dragon
(Ctenophorus fordi)
Southern Hairy-nosed Wombat
(Lasiorhinus latifrons)
Desert Banded Snake
(Simoselaps bertholdi)
Spinifex Hopping Mouse
(Notomys alexis)

One Million Years Ago

A million years ago the Nullarbor Plain was a vastly different place, as it was covered with a large variety of trees and plants. It was home to many strange kinds of mammals, birds and reptiles, some of which resemble animals living today, like kangaroos, wombats and koalas, and others that looked very different.

The largest of these strange animals were called the 'megafauna' (from the Greek 'mega', meaning 'big'). Such beasts once roamed all of Australia. They included giant kangaroos up to three metres high, like *Procoptodon goliath,* a giant wombat-like animal called *Diprotodon*, a gargantuan flightless bird called *Genyornis* and a six metre long goanna, *Megalania*.

The giant mammals were mostly plant-eaters that browsed on leaves or ate grasses. All that is, except one, the hunter of the group. This beast was Australia's equivalent of the African lion or the Asian tiger, except that it was a marsupial, with a pouch for its young. This is why, when scientists first studied its bones in 1859, it was dubbed the 'marsupial lion'. Its scientific name, *Thylacoleo carnifex*, actually means 'pouched lion that eats flesh'.

This story follows the tale of one such animal that lived on the Nullabor Plain about a million years ago. We will call him Leo.

The Life and Times of Leo

Leo was born as one of a small litter of baby marsupial lions. As a tiny foetus he crawled out of his mother's womb and entered her pouch where he attached himself to one of her teats. From here he could drink as much milk as he wanted, and sleep and grow. Life was blissfully simple until he woke up one day to realise that he had grown too big for his mother's pouch!

Leo had been sharing the pouch with two of his siblings, Leanna, his sister, and Lionel, his brother. On the big day when they were kicked out of home, they learned that the outside world was a scary place for young marsupial lions. At first they stayed very close to their mother, while she hunted for food for them. She would catch a kangaroo or a possum and they loved to chew on the bones and slice off pieces of meat with their razor-sharp teeth.

Gradually Leo and his siblings grew braver and began wandering away from their mother to explore the new world on their own.

They had learned that small animals feared them and ran away. They also learned to hide from larger animals, especially other marsupial lions, or the large striped marsupial tigers (*thylacines*). They also had to watch for giant snakes and goannas, but luckily these were very rare in that part of Australia.

Soon the three young marsupial lions started to hunt for themselves. They began by playing hunting games, creeping up slowly and silently and springing surprise attacks on each other. Eventually they each learned how to creep up on other animals and kill them for food.

As the three young lions became expert hunters they grew much larger and each wandered off on its own way, as they could hunt better by themselves. Leo learned to love life alone on the land. He enjoyed nothing better than a big meal of freshly killed giant short-faced kangaroo.

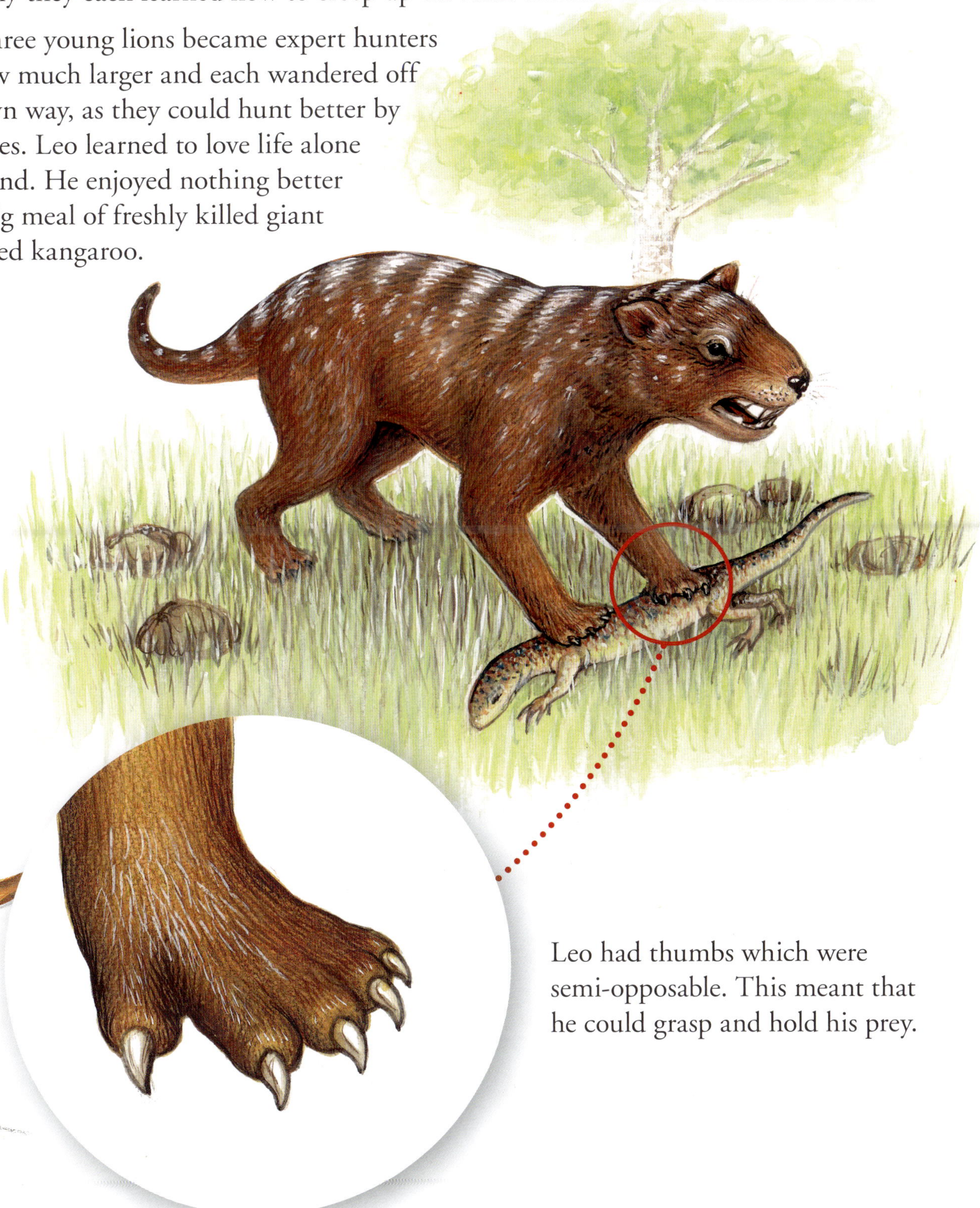

Leo had thumbs which were semi-opposable. This meant that he could grasp and hold his prey.

Leo's Tragic Adventure

One day Leo was stalking a mob of giant kangaroos. Quietly, he crept along on his belly, hidden from the kangaroos by a large, fallen log. His plan was to get as close as possible to the mob, which were browsing on the tender leaves of a small salmon gum tree, then pounce on the nearest one.

He was almost upon them, when he accidentally stepped on a dry twig, snapping the tiny branch. The kangaroos stopped eating, turning their heads towards the sound. One of them sniffed the air and caught a whiff of hungry lion. They bolted away at once.

Leo sprang from behind the log and gave chase. He was steadily gaining on one of the big bounders, running as fast as his legs could carry him. As the big roo turned left, Leo quickly threw himself left and was almost upon the hopping meal when suddenly, unexpectedly, he felt the ground disappear below his feet.

Crash! His jaw hit a ledge of rock, his feet dangled in mid air. He was in the mouth of a cave, a vertical drop that went down and down into blackness. Moments later he crashed down with a massive thud. He was at the bottom of a very large cave. His chin and legs ached, but were not broken.

Leo looked up and could see a small circle of sky way above him. Light filtered down to a small area below the cave entrance. With no way to climb the many metres to the hole above, Leo thought the only thing he could do was explore the cave and find another way out.

The cave floor was full of interesting smells for a marsupial lion. There were many skeletons and dried carcasses of animals, mostly kangaroos. He gnawed on one skeleton and chewed the dried sinews on the bones. It wasn't much of a meal; he preferred fresh meat, not dried jerky.

He explored the cave in the pitch darkness, wandering a long way away from the entrance. He found no food of any kind, only a little water along the side of the cave wall that had dribbled down from above.

As time passed Leo grew weak from lack of food and thirsty once the water source had dried up. Eventually, after trying every nook and cranny in the cave for a way out without success, he gave up. He lay down and went into a deep sleep. He dreamed of his brother, sister and mother and happy times playing hunting games.

He died there in the cave — but that is not the end of his story. For there is life after death once you become a fossil!

Leo's bones on the cave floor.

Leo Becomes a Fossil

Leo's body lay there as if he was sleeping. Flies flew in and laid eggs on his carcass and the maggots eventually ate away all his soft tissue, leaving only his skin and white bones. His body became mummified for a while, retaining its skin with colour patterns. As more time passed tiny bacteria began to slowly eat up all the dried parts of his skin and hair.

After several thousands of years, Leo's skeleton was all that was left of him. It lay there at the bottom of the cave, still in the same position in which he went to sleep, his arms curled underneath his head.

Hundreds of thousands of years passed. The only action to take place in the cave was an occasional earth tremor that shook the cave lightly for a few seconds each time. This shaking moved apart some of the smaller bones in Leo's hands, feet and tail.

While Leo's skeleton lay there in the pitch dark, many other animals fell into the cave. Each would roam around searching for food and water, but they also would eventually die. One day a curious dingo fell into the cave and walked over Leo's skeleton, breaking some of his rib bones. The dingo then lay down about 20 metres away from Leo and slept for the last time.

The cave breathed each day as the air pressure below the ground changed. Much fine dust and sand drifted into the cave from its entrance, but the gentle movements of air from the changing air pressues prevented any build up of dust on Leo's skeleton. Eventually the entrance became blocked up with drifting branches and mud flowing in from the heavy winter floods.

Though Leo had died his remains had become a fossil. A million years passed after Leo's death before the cave would be discovered again.

Dingo footprints in Leo's cave.

Modern Exploration on the Nullarbor

In April 2002 a team of cave explorers came out to search the Nullarbor Plain. They loved nothing better than finding and exploring new caves.

The cavers set up a camp on the Plain and each day when the weather was fine an ultra light aircraft called 'Flightstar' would take to the sky, piloted by Ken Boland. As he flew over the limestone plain, if he spotted holes in the ground he clicked his satellite-positioning device, a GPS (Global Positioning System), to record their exact location.

Then teams with four-wheel drive vehicles would use the information from the GPS to drive out and explore the new caves.

The expedition arriving on the Nullarbor.

The campsite on the plain.

The ultralight 'Flightstar'.

Finding the Fossil

One day they found a new cave that appeared to be a deep round hole. Ken Boland and Ray Gibbons were the first to explore it. They dropped down the hole on ropes, discovering it was 18 metres from the top to the cave floor.

Descending into the cave.

With head lamps turned on and torches in hand they slowly walked around the cave. All about them were the dried carcasses of kangaroos and birds. Eventually they came to the deepest end of the cave, about 70 metres from the surface of the ground.

They walked slowly, taking care not to step on any bones. Crawling under a rocky ledge on hands and knees, they emerged into another new chamber.

One of them shone his torch around and was surprised to see a glistening white skeleton. Its huge head bore long, sharp teeth. They knew at once that it was not an animal from recent times but something that had died a very long, long time ago — something prehistoric!

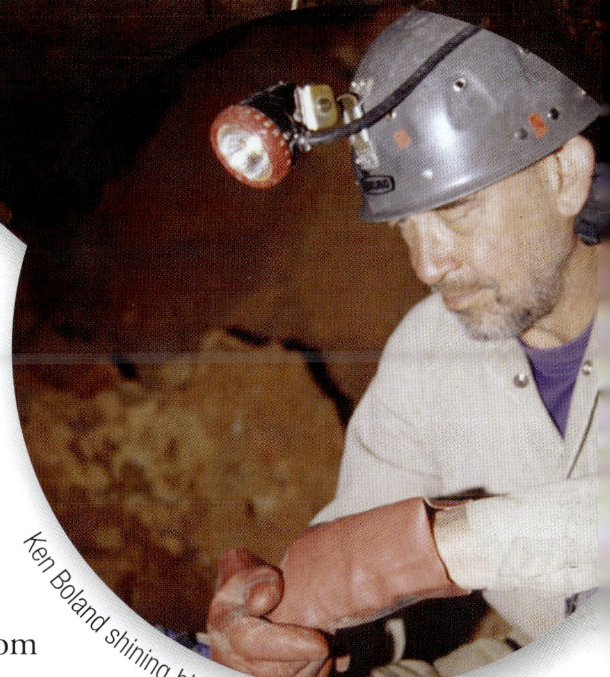

Ken Boland shining his torch onto the cave floor.

The cavers took photographs of the fossil but didn't get too close as they thought it might be something very special that scientists would want to study without any contamination from their presence.

Back at camp Ken and Ray told the other cavers their exciting news. When the trip had finished they all returned home to different cities; some lived in Adelaide, some in Melbourne and others in Perth. The leaders of the group contacted experts in the Melbourne Museum with news of the great discovery.

The news of the great fossil find spread among the scientists in the various state museums but as the find was in Western Australia, it was the Western Australian Museum that was privileged to organise an expedition and recover the fossils.

The Expedition

In July 2002 a team of scientists from the Western Australian Museum and Flinders University met up with the cavers on the Nullarbor Plain, and were led to the site where Leo had been found.

It was an exciting moment for the scientists, as they were able to confirm that the cavers had indeed found the first ever complete, perfect skeleton of a marsupial lion!

The first job was to mark off the fossil site with yellow tape so as to keep people away from the discovery. Then one of the scientists put on a white suit with rubber gloves and a mask, not to keep him clean but to ensure the skeleton site was not contaminated with fibres, hair or other substances from his body and clothing. He walked carefully to the skeleton, bent down, and began to take samples of the bones to test for remains of ancient DNA. DNA is a molecule found in all living things and is unique to each species.

The samples would then be analysed in a laboratory to see if any traces of Leo's DNA remained.

Sampling for ancient DNA.

Preparing the fossil with a soft brush.

Then the job of preserving Leo's skeleton began. The scientists carefully coated Leo's bones with a penetrating glue that soaked into the bone and hardened it from the inside. They took a week to do this and to let the skeleton dry before it was ready to be moved. After photographs were taken showing the skeleton's position, each bone was carefully wrapped in tissue paper and packed in a plastic drum. The drum was then carefully pulled up out of the cave by rope.

John Long (left) and Carmelo Amelfi (right) applying glue to harden Leo's bones.

Carefully pulling up fossils from the cave.

New Discoveries

While two of the scientists had been busy hardening Leo's skeleton, the other scientists explored the rest of the cave and nearby caves. During the course of the two-week expedition the team found another seven nearly complete skeletons of marsupial lions. They also found complete skeletons of fossil kangaroos, giant wombats and parts of skeletons of many other kinds of prehistoric animals and birds.

Many strange kinds of kangaroos were discovered. One small wallaby had strange bony bumps over its eyes and a deep narrow snout. This small wallaby represents something new to science.

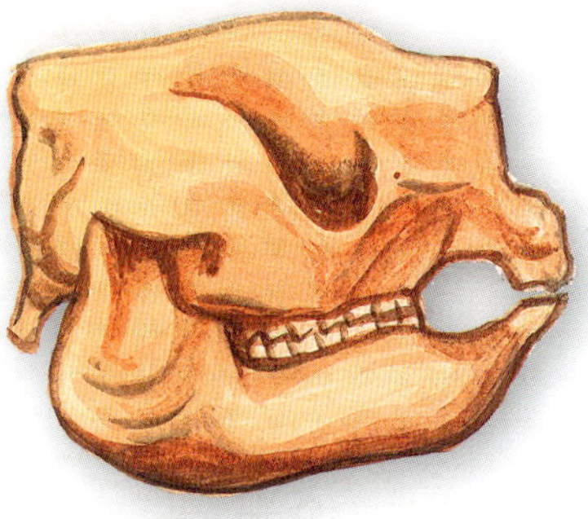

Procoptodon skull

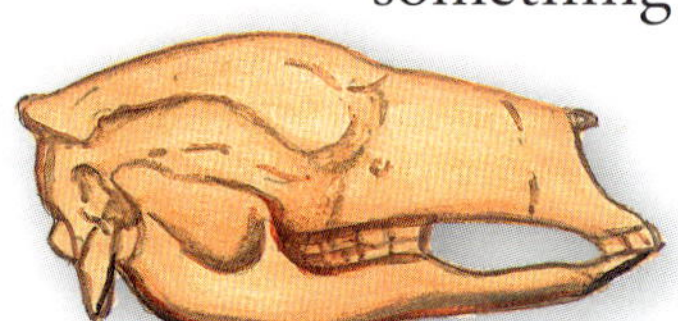

Modern kangaroo skull

Procoptodon

Other fossil kangaroos included the short-faced forms called *Sthenurus*, the giant *Procoptodon*, and a huge wallaby called *Protemnodon*. One of the most unexpected creatures the team found was the remains of a tree kangaroo. This proves that trees once covered the Nullarbor when Leo and his fellow animals were alive.

The skull of a new kind of kangaroo found in Leo's Nullarbor cave.

An artists impression of what the new kind kangaroo may have looked like.

The team of scientists and cavers went back and explored the caves over three years. They recovered many skeletons belonging to some 30 different kinds of animals and birds. The sites were far richer than anyone ever imagined, as many bones were found by searching under rock piles and digging in sediment within the cave floors.

Mummified bird carcass.

The skull of the extinct kangaroo *Sthenurus* being prepared on the cave floor.

Finding out about Leo

Once Leo's bones and those of the other marsupial lions were back at the Western Australian Museum the scientists could begin to study them. Their aim was to find out what he looked like and how he lived.

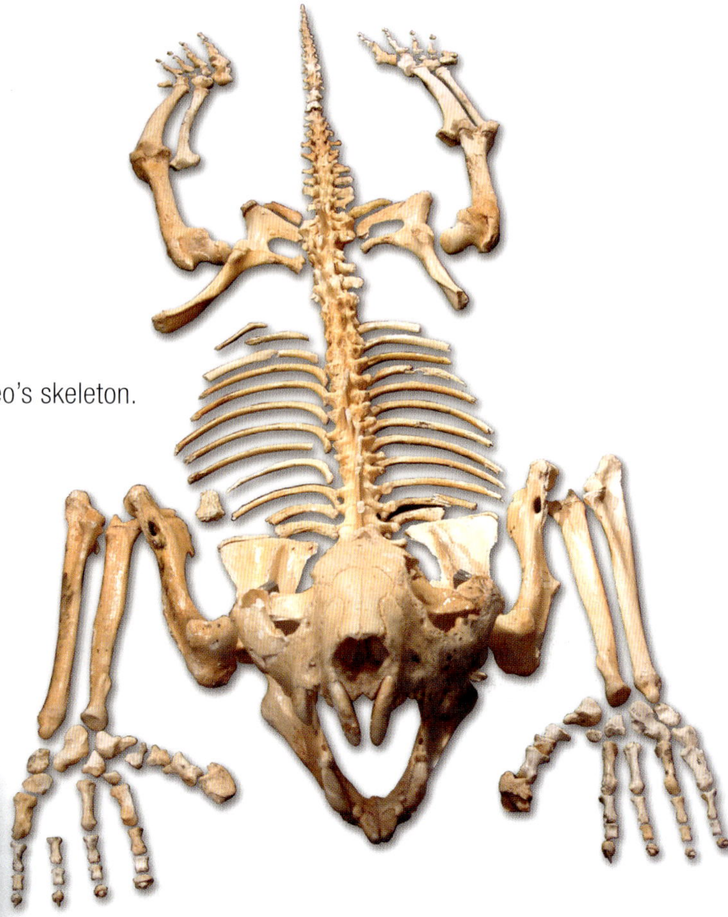

Leo's skeleton.

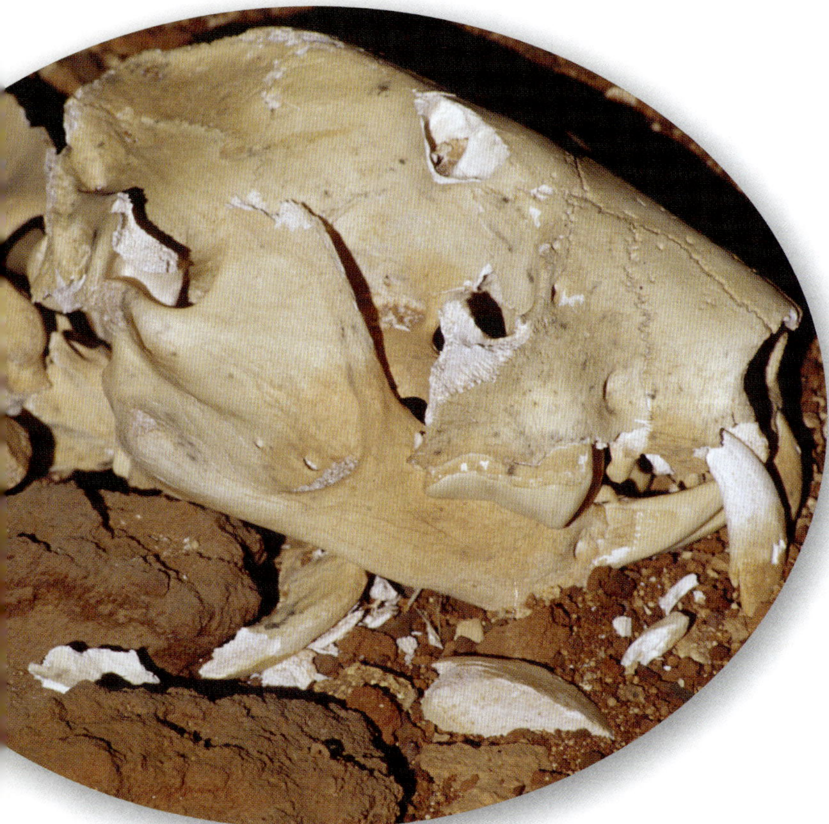

A restored marsupial lion skeleton from Naracoorte Caves, South Australia. This restoration is actually made up from many isolated bones from different animals, so it is a best guess of how the marsupial lion skeleton looked.

How do we know what Leo looked like?

First the scientists put Leo's skeleton back together, using the photographs of how he was discovered. This is called natural articulation. The skeleton shows what Leo's overall shape must have been like.

Next, using the muscle patterns common to all marsupials, an artist drew Leo with muscles and ligaments added to the bones. Each bone shows where its muscles attached and the thickness of each bone reflects how large the animal's muscles must have been.

Finally, using colour patterns from modern day marsupials the artist imagines what Leo could have looked like. The artist and scientist discuss what the land, vegetation and climate could have been like when Leo lived and how his colouring would camouflage him for hunting and from predators and in this way they come up with a likely colour pattern for him. They will not know for certain but it is based on well-informed guesswork.

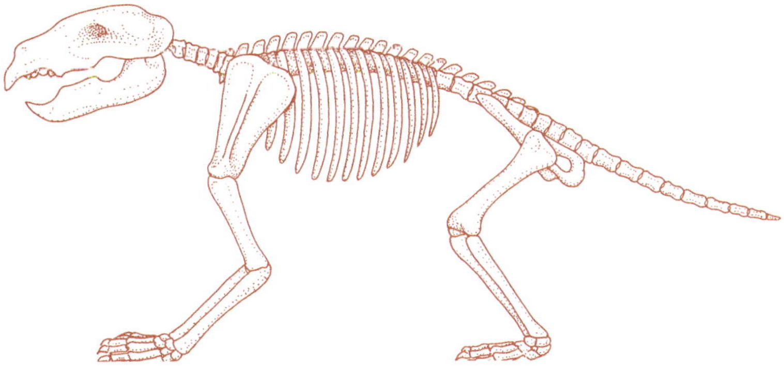

Leo's skeleton.

Leo's skeleton with muscles and ligaments added.

Thylacoleo carnifex

Tasmanian Tiger
(Thylacinus cynocephalus)

Spotted-tailed Quoll
(Dasyurus maculatus)

Numbat
(Myrmecobius fasciatus)

How do we know what Leo ate?

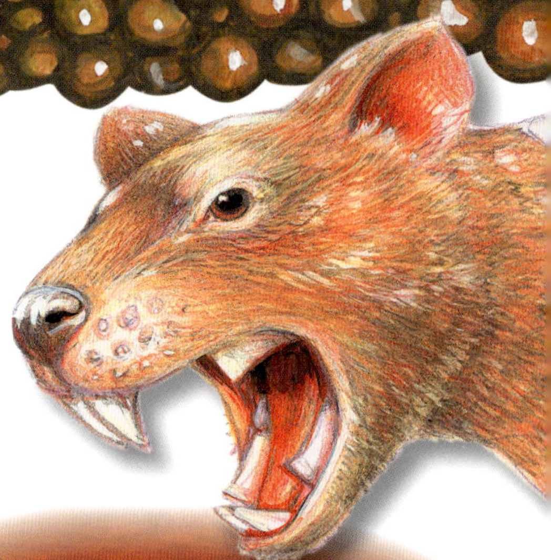

The type of food an animal eats is indicated by its teeth. Animals that eat plants, like cows or kangaroos, tend to have broad, grinding teeth, whereas flesh-eaters, like lions and dogs, tend to have sharp teeth with pointed fangs.

Leo had amazing teeth that were unlike any other creature on Earth. His front teeth, called incisors, were large, sharp fangs with serrated outer edges, like steak knives. His cheek teeth were enlarged to fill most of the biting area. These shearing teeth are called premolars.

Leo had enormous upper and lower premolars that slid past each other to slice like gardening shears. The jaws were powerful enough to slice big chunks of meat off the large animals he fed upon.

There is also one other clue to what Leo ate. When his teeth are examined under a high-powered microscope we can see tiny scratches and grooves formed from bone splinters scratching his teeth. This proves he ate mostly other animals.

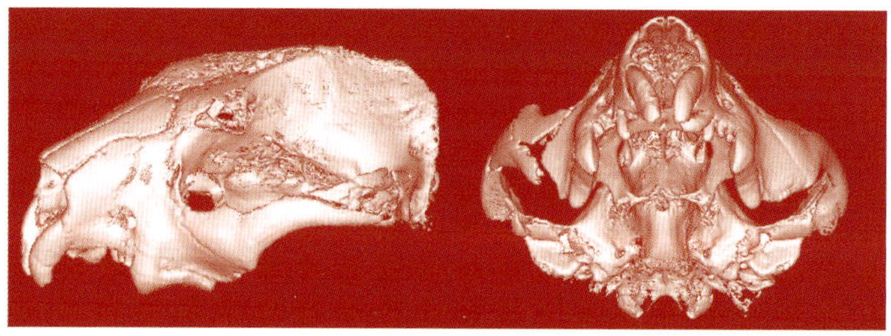

Computer generated images of Leo's skull using a CT scanner.

How long ago did Leo live?

Some of the bones of the other marsupial lions found in the caves had crystals of cave rock growing over them.

Scientists at Melbourne University were able to analyse the gypsum crystals for tiny inclusions that indicated how long the crystals had been growing.

Other methods such as dating the cave floor sands and looking at radioactive atoms within the bones and teeth of the fossils give a crosscheck on the age of the fossils. By using all these methods together we can estimate that Leo's bones and the other fossils are probably between 500,000 and 1 million years old.

Staglagmites growing up from the cave floor take thousands of years to form.

THE GEOLOGICAL TIME SCALE

Eon	Era	Period	Time	Events
Phanerozoic Eon	Cainozoic era	Quaternary	Recent	
			0.01 million years ago	
			Pleistocene	*Thylacoleo* and Megafauna extinctions
		Tertiary	1.6 million years ago	
			Pliocene	Appearance of humans
			5 million years ago	
			Miocene	*Wakaleo*
			25 million years ago	*Priscileo*
			Oligocene	
			45 million years ago	
			Eocene	First whales
			57 million years ago	
			Palaeocene	Extinction of dinosaurs
	Mesozoic Era		66.4 million years ago	
			Cretaceous	Australia's oldest mammal
			144 million years ago	
			Jurassic	First birds
			208 million years ago	
			Triassic	First mammals and dinosaurs; Many extinctions
	Palaeozoic Era		245 million years ago	
			Permian	
			286 million years ago	First mammal-like reptiles
			Carboniferous	First reptiles
			355 million years ago	
			Devonian	First amphibians
			408 million years ago	
			Silurian	First jawed fishes
			438 million years ago	
			Ordovician	
			510 million years ago	First vertebrates — jawless fishes
			Cambrian	Invertebrates diverse and abundant
	Precambrian Era		540 million years ago	
			Proterozoic	First many celled creatures
			2500 million years ago	
			Archaean	Oldest life on earth. 3.5 billion year old stromatolites
			4500 million years ago	

Where did Leo come from?

Marsupial lions are a group of animals that died out a long time ago and have no close living relatives. However, fossils that date back to more than 25 million years ago show us that the first marsupial lions such as *Priscileo* were small animals, more like marsupial pussycats.

Priscileo evolved from either a possum-like ancestor or an ancient relative of wombats.

Wakaleo was a medium-sized marsupial lion the size of a kelpie. It lived about 10 million years ago. It, too, had large slicing premolar teeth but they were not as large as those in *Thylacoleo*.

Thylacoleo first appeared about 4 million years ago and the first species, *Thylacoleo hilli*, was quite small, about the size of a cat. Other species of *Thylacoleo* were much larger, such as *Thylacoleo crassicaudatus*, the size of a large dog. *Thylacoleo carnifex*, was the biggest of all marsupial lions. It grew to 1.6 metres long and weighed around 100 kg — about the length of a panther, but much bulkier.

The Great Unsolved Mystery

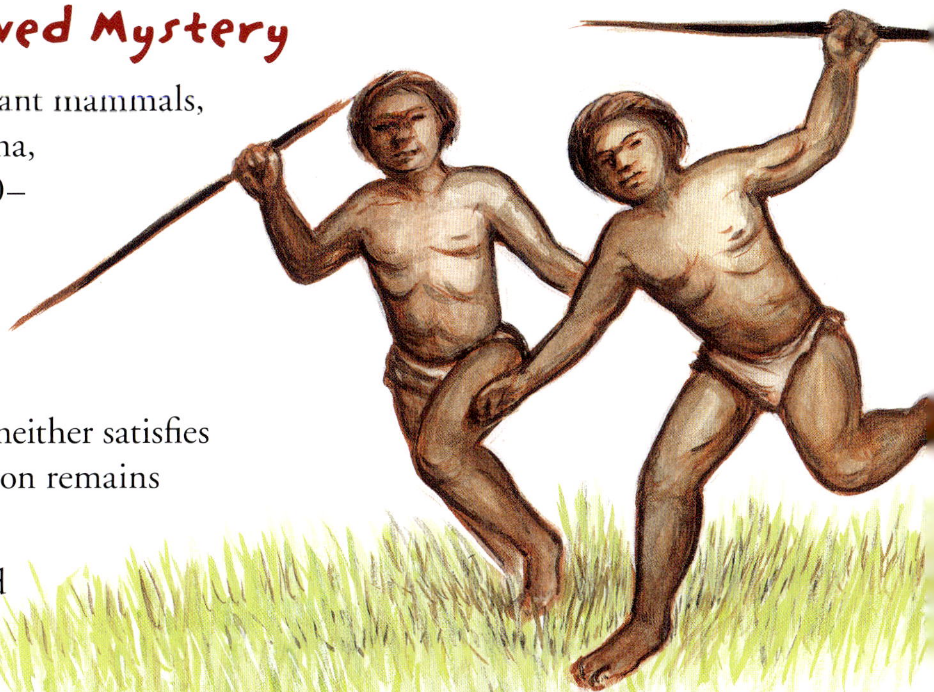

Leo, the marsupial lion, and all the giant mammals, birds and reptiles, called the megafauna, mysteriously died out between 50,000–40,000 years ago. Yet other animals, such as today's kangaroos, wombats and koalas live on. Why did the megafauna suddenly disappear?

Scientists have two explanations, but neither satisfies all the evidence we have, so the question remains unsolved.

One explanation is that people arrived in Australia around 60,000 years ago and began hunting the biggest animals for food. After thousands of years of hunting and setting fire to the bush to catch animals, the landscape changed and could no longer feed enough of the larger animals, so they died out.

The other explanation is that gradual changes in climate, including several cold periods called 'ice ages' meant that the plants couldn't grow as abundantly as in the past warmer climates. The largest animals could not find enough food to eat, so they died out and with them went the large meat-eaters.

Perhaps the real answer is that both of these explanations are true, neither one is correct entirely on its own.

The Legend of Leo Lives On

Today you can see bones of marsupial lions on display at all of the major museums throughout Australia and at some other special places like the Naracoorte Visitor Centre in South Australia.

Leo is also well known as a star of television, including on the ABC 'Catalyst' program.

A Japanese film company filmed the teams collecting fossils in the Nullarbor caves and then made a computer graphic reconstruction of Leo as a live animal. It was the first time a marsupial lion had been brought to life on the television screen and it was shown to over 20 million people.

Leo is now world famous. His bones are well looked after in the Western Australian Museum and in the 'Diamonds to Dinosaurs' gallery you can see his skull on display with his mouth open, showing his big teeth. Come and see him any day — he is there waiting for you.

Glossary and pronunciation guide

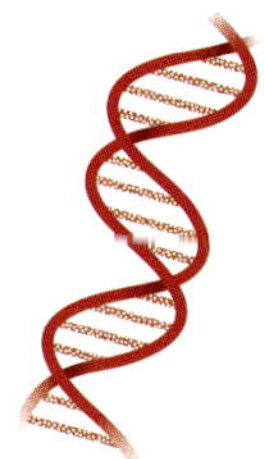

DNA
Stands for deoxyribonucleic acid, the basic building block of life. Found inside our cells, its pattern is unique to every living and fossil species.

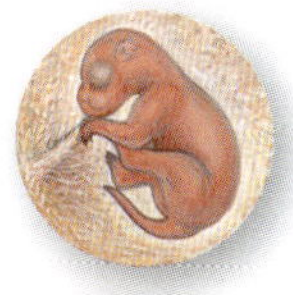

Foetus (fee-tuss)
Unborn young of a living animal.

Fossil (foss-ill)
The physical remains of past life on the planet, such as bones, plants, or wood, or even traces of animals such as footprints.

Genyornis (Jenny-or-niss)
A giant flightless bird of the Pleistocene–Pliocene Periods.

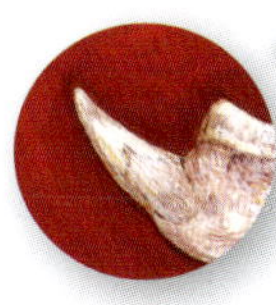

Incisor (in-sigh-zor)
The front cutting teeth of a mammal.

Limestone
Rock made up mostly of calcium carbonate (mainly shell pieces and silts). Caves form commonly in limestone rock.

Marsupial (mar-soup-ee-al)
A kind of mammal that gives birth to very small young which develop in the mother's pouch.

Megalania (meg-a-lane-ee-ar)
A giant extinct goanna that reached up to 6 metres long and roamed around Australia during the Pleistocene Period.

Priscileo (priss-key-lee-o)
A small marsupial lion the size of a cat. It lived about 25 million years ago.

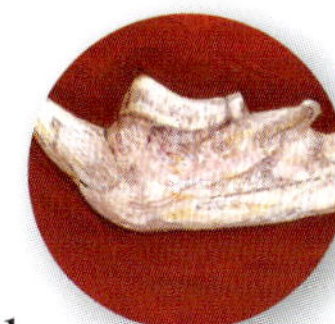

Premolar (pre-mole-ar)
One of the teeth in the cheek of all mammals, behind the front cutting teeth (incisors and canines) but in front of the grinding molar teeth.

Procoptodon (pro-cop-toe-don)
The largest kangaroo that ever lived (up to 2.5 metres high); Pleistocene Period.

Stalagmite (stal-ag-mite)
Stalagmites are formed by calcium rich water dripping on to the cave floor, building up a tall strture of calcium carbonate over many years. Stalactites (stal-ac-tites) are similar but grow down from the cave roof.

Sthenurus (ss-then-you-russ)
Large short-faced kangaroos of the Pleistocene–Pliocene Periods.

Thylacine (thigh-la-seen)
Tasmaina Tiger, a wolf-like marsupial predator, only recently extinct in Tasmania.

Thylacoleo (thigh-lack-o-lee-o)
Mostly large marsupial lion of the Pleistocene–Pliocene Periods.

Wakaleo (wack-a-lee-o)
A medium-sized marsupial lion that lived in the Miocene–Pliocene periods.

About the author

Dr John Long was Curator of Vertebrate Palaeontology at the Western Australian Museum between 1989–2004, and is currently head of Sciences at Museum Victoria. He is the author of several books on prehistory for both children and adults, including *Gogo Fish! The Story of the Western Australian Fossil Emblem* (Western Australian Museum, 2004) and *The Big Picture Book* (Allen & Unwin, 2005).

About the illustrator

Jill Ruse is a graphic designer and illustrator with over thirty years of experience. She has illustrated a variety of projects for the Western Australian Museum over the years. Her previous picture book with John Long *Gogo Fish! The Story of the Western Australian Fossil Emblem* was an Honour Book in the 2005 Children's Book Council of Australia Awards.

First Published 2009 by the
Western Australian Museum
49 Kew Street
Welshpool, Western Australia 6106
www.museum.wa.gov.au

Designed by Cathie Glassby and Michael Neiman
Editor Jane Hammond Foster
Printed by South Wind Productions, Singapore

Page 17: GPS photo ©iStockphoto.com/bartekpiaski
Page 19: Compass photo ©iStockphoto.com/Nikada
Page 20: Horned Kangaroo reconstruction by J.Long.
Page 24: CT scan images by Mark Walter, PMH, Perth.

National Library of Australia
Cataloguing-in-publication entry

Long, John A., 1957-
The short tragic life of Leo the marsupial lion / John Long ; illustrator, Jill Ruse.

1st ed.
ISBN: 9781920843946 (hb)

Subjects
I. Thylacoleo — Nullarbor Plain (S. Aust. and W.A.)—Juvenile literature. II. Paleontology — Nullarbor Plain (S. Aust. and W.A.) — Juvenile literature. III. Paleontology — Pleistocene — Juvenile literature. IV. Mammals, fossil — Nullarbor Plain (S. Aust and W.A.)— Juvenile literature. V. Nullarbor Plain (S. Aust. and W.A.) — Juvenile literature.

Ruse, Jill.

599.270994